Imagination

Written by Clancy L. Mullenaux

Illustrated by Shayla R. Allred

AuthorHouse™
1663 Liberty Drive
Bloomington, IN 47403
www.authorhouse.com
Phone: 833-262-8899

Because of the dynamic nature of the Internet, any web addresses or links contained in this book may have changed
since publication and may no longer be valid. The views expressed in this work are solely those of the author and do not
necessarily reflect the views of the publisher, and the publisher hereby disclaims any responsibility for them.

Any people depicted in stock imagery provided by Getty Images are models,
and such images are being used for illustrative purposes only.
Certain stock imagery © Getty Images.

This book is printed on acid-free paper.

ISBN: 978-1-6655-3888-6 (sc)
ISBN: 978-1-6655-3887-9 (hc)
ISBN: 978-1-6655-3889-3 (e)

Library of Congress Control Number: 2021919348

Print information available on the last page.

Published by AuthorHouse 09/23/2021

authorHOUSE®

CONTENTS

DON'T BE A CHICKEN, TOM

Farmer John just got done packing up his chicken eggs to send to Indiana. When he got to Farmer Bill's in Indiana he put them into a warm box to hatch. After a week they finally hatched. Farmer Bill noticed one chick was bigger. He named him Tom; he didn't fit in. Every time the chickens jumped on their roost they said "come on Tom," he said "what if I fall?" they replied "don't be a chicken, Tom." When the chickens went into the egg box they said "come in Tom," he said "what if I get stuck," they replied "don't be a chicken, Tom." Every time they ate they said "come eat Tom." He said "what if I get poisoned," they replied "don't be a chicken, Tom." Days passed, but one morning they saw a different farmer. It was farmer John. He said "that's a big chicken you have there, can I take him to my place?". Farmer Bill said "sure." When Tom arrived he recognized two of the turkeys who came up to him and they also recognized him and they realized that Tom was home. They were his parents. He was so happy they only said to him "Be yourself."

TREV'S JOURNEY

Trey is a triceratops. He was walking with his parents when an asteroid crashed down. His parents died and so he started to run back to his house. On his way he saw a long neck and asked "what's your name?" The long neck replied "Larry, what's yours?" He said "mine is Trey." And they both started running to Trey's house. They got lost in a forest. Trey thought they were going to die. For a while they ate leaves and then Trey figured out where to go. They were on the trail when they heard a rumbling in the bushes. They were so scared! A stegosaurus came out and they asked "what's your name?" She said "Stacy, what's yours?" They said, "Mine is Trey and mine's Larry." They all started walking to Trey's house. They crossed a river and all the fish were tickling Larry's feet. Then they had to cross a mountain, when Stacy tripped and got hurt, so they decided to rest there. In the morning they finally got to Trey's house. Trey was so happy he ran inside. There they played games and had a lot of fun. Trey was very happy with his new family.

WILSON'S TRIP

Wilson is a man from 3048. He was smart, so he brought a time machine and a few tools. He got all done packing and left on his trip. He was driving his car deep in the desert when his car ran out of gas. Good thing he was prepared for this. He got his time machine and went back to the time of the dinosaur extinction, found a dinosaur and ran into the time machine and went back to 3048. Went to the place he saw the dinosaur and started to dig. He dug for a while and then found oil. Then he got some of his tools and took apart the time machine. Then he rebuilt it into a machine that turns oil into gas. He got that oil and turned it into gas. It took a long time but he got the gas, filled his car and continued his trip. He had so much fun. He went on roller coasters, and went to see new movies, and went shopping and got a hover car. Wilson drove to a different place where he went to a museum, and to the best restaurant in town. Wilson had so much fun he stayed for a few more days!

DAN AND DUSTY

Dan is a dog who was lost in the woods. He barked for a very long time. When he heard something bark back he went to where he heard the sound but nothing was there. He heard it again but nothing was there. Then he went farther and saw a hound. The hound told him to come to the farm with him. He followed the hound and was excited to have a home, but it wasn't long before Dan and the hound started fighting over who was a better dog. Many days passed and they were still fighting! Dusty the horse was also lost when he came to the farm. He met another horse, then they started fighting. They fought for a long time over who was a better horse. Dan and Dusty were both tired of fighting. That night they went to the edge of the fence and saw each other, Dan asked Dusty "what is your name?" Dusty said "Dusty, what's yours?" Dan said "mines Dan." Soon they became friends and figured out that they both came to the farm as lost animals. Dan and Dusty went on fun adventures together.

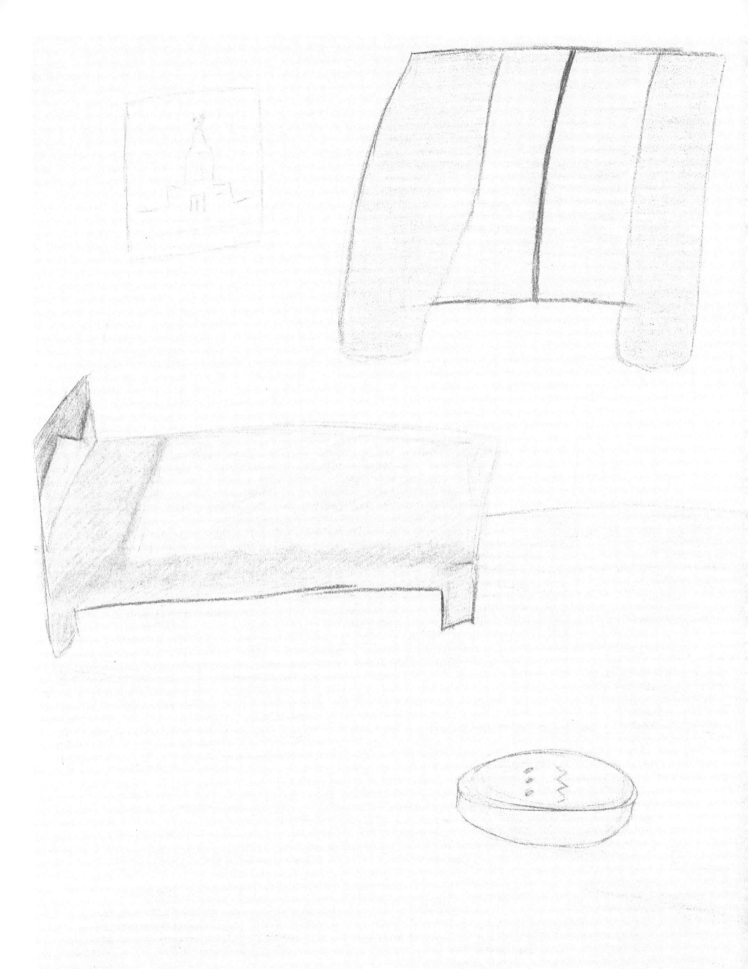

VICTOR'S FRIENDS

Victor is a robot vacuum, and he vacuums the kids' rooms at night. These rooms have special friends of his. In the little sister's room there is a doll, and they like to talk about secrets such as "once I let all the dust go in the pantry." The doll said "once I hid in the closet for two days." When they were all done he went into the little brother's room. There he told jokes with the teddy bear. Victor said "why aren't ghosts popular at parties," Teddy said "I don't know, why?" Victor said "because they always bring a BOO!" They both started laughing. Then they started telling other jokes. After a bit Victor went to the older sister's room. There he found a lava lamp and they did makeup. Victor said "I would like a makeover please," he giggled. By the end he looked like a clown. Then it was time to go to the older brother's room. It took him a while to find the computer but he finally did and they played games and told stories. It was lots of fun but morning was coming, so Victor went back to cleaning. He likes to play and joke with his friends at night.

ROB THE ROBOT

Rob is a robot that is controlled by Dr. Allred. He made Rob destroy other robots. Rob didn't like this job. He made a master plan that one day he would turn on Dr. Allred. Rob always went out at night and gathered other robots to help him. One day the Dr. figured out that Rob was sneaking out at night, so the Dr. made a machine that would destroy Rob. It had lasers, ice cannons, and gas bombs. The next day the Dr. put a tracker on Rob and kicked him out. The Dr. knew exactly where Rob was. One day Rob was in the park playing with his friends when all the sudden a GIANT MACHINE came out of the ground! Rob was surprised to see this, luckily his friends were right there to help him. They started fighting, but Dr. Allred shot all his gas bombs. but this didn't affect the robots. Next he launched his ice balls, but one of his friends had fire guns. He melted the ice balls then he shot his lasers. Rob got a huge mirror, and it reflected into the machine. Dr. Allred lost the battle. Rob and his friends were super happy.

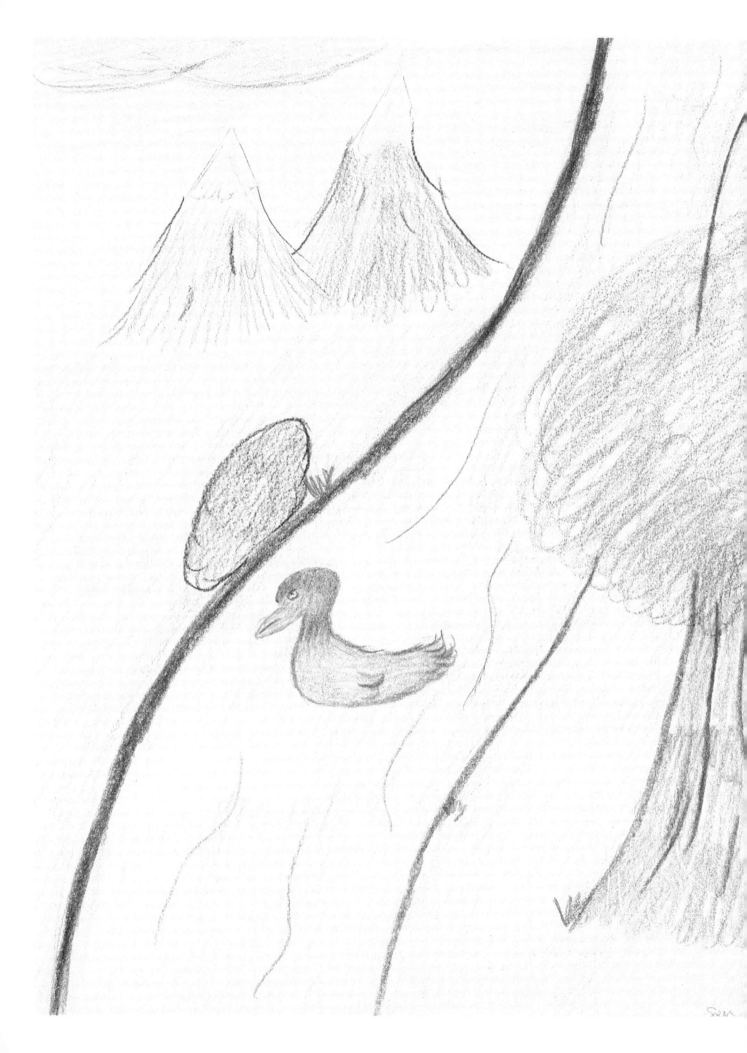

DORKUS THE DUCK

Dorkus is a duck. He always got made fun of. This made him very angry and sad, so he never talked to anyone. The salamander said "hey Dorkus got any dork friends, oh wait you don't have any hahahahahaha!" and the fish would say "your name is dumb." Dorkus wanted to cry but then the fish said "are you going to cry, you're a baby?" Dorkus decided to run away. The rest of the animals now had no one to pick on. It had been many days he had been gone.

Dorkus was swimming around when he saw a flood! He swam as fast as he could until he reached home. He grabbed salamander and threw him on land. Then grabbed a jar filled it up with water and put all the fish in and pulled the jar out. But it was too late, he got swept away and the other animals felt so bad. They were crying, but then one of the fish had an idea! They traveled down the river still feeling bad. They traveled for one full day, finally the salamander said "I see him!" Dorkus was hurt really bad, but they helped him get better. One of the fish said "you're a legend."

UNDERWATER WAR

Neva is a mermaid that controls half of the oceans. Her twin brother rules the other half, but he wants to rule her half as well. Her brother's name is Aven. He was planning to one day take over the oceans. Finally, it was time for Aven to take over the seas. He went to Neva's kingdom. He tricked her into leaving the palace. Neva knew Aven was just trying to take over the seas. She hid behind a wall of sand, and started creeping up on him. The fight began, and they started using powers. They fought for many days. In the end Neva won! The whole kingdom was happy for her. They decided to throw a party with super good juice and food. She had so much fun with her family. This was not the end. Her son and her daughter were now the king and queen of the oceans. Neva is old now, but luckily her children made it all one kingdom. Everyone is happy this way.

THE LOST CITY OF ATLANTIS

Waylon is a hammerhead shark. He loved adventuring and going to places like Japan, the Bahamas, and Fiji. One day, Waylon was swimming below Spain and above Africa. He saw something really bright. He followed the light and he found a chunk of the earth. Waylon thought back to when he was in Japan. He saw a sign that said "The Lost City Of Atlantis." He knew what it meant by "lost." He had found the lost city of Atlantis! Waylon went inside. It was super bright, but soon his eyes adjusted. Waylon saw everything. There were games, vending machines, and lots of fish and other sharks like him. There was even an underwater volcano! It exploded underwater, so it didn't do much but it was cool and it made the water warmer. He also went to parties and played games. Then he saw a kingdom and went inside and saw Neva, the mermaid. They became best friends and played games. Soon it was time for Waylon to go back home to the Caribbean Islands.

GARDEN FRIENDS

Delani is a scarecrow; she loves talking to others. One day she saw something round and orange. She went over and said "Hello, anyone there?" It was a pumpkin. He said "Hi my name is Gavin. What's yours?" "Mine's Delani," she said. They played many games and read together. They had so much fun, but then they heard a rustling in the bushes. They looked over and saw a squirrel. They said "Hi, you look fun and nice. Our names are Delani and Gavin. What's yours?" The squirrel said, "Mine's Stacy. Mind if I join your group?" They replied "Of course you can!" They had a lot of fun going on adventures and trips. The fun felt like it would never end! Gavin got sick, and he was so sad he thought he would never see his friends again. Delani brought him soup and medicine. He was so happy they played a couple games. Stacy brought some cake, and they all had a little party. Delani had so much fun with her friends and was very happy to be with them. Friends are great!

KING OF THE LIONS

Logan was the king of the lions. He was a great king. All the lions liked him as king. One day he got news that there was trouble in the east. Logan went to see what it was. There was a pack of leopards who were planning to take over the land that was owned by Logan! Lucky for him he kept quiet. He went back to his den kind of scared. He decided to attack tomorrow. The next day he was ready to charge with his army. He said "We charge on three! ONE! TWO! THREE!" They all ran east. The leopards saw this and became frightened they got together an army as fast as they could. Then they charged west. Both teams were a little scared. If you didn't know, fear makes doing anything harder. Logan knew that, so he left his fear behind and picked up courage. They both fought for days, and it was very tiring. They took breaks, but in the end Logan won! He was very happy and they lived in peace from then on. Remember don't have fear; it only makes things worse. Only have courage; it helps a lot.

DEEP IN SPACE

Zara was a person on Earth. She loved Legos and mac and cheese. She was at the park with her friends when a huge thing from the sky was falling down. Her friends ran to their parents. The huge thing was coming fast. It crashed right by her, she was so scared! When the dust settled, she realized it was a spaceship from a different planet, and she loved space. Zara looked inside, and no one was in there-or so she thought. When she was flying the spaceship out of the atmosphere, she heard a whisper. So she stopped, and started looking around, and asked "Who is there?" She looked closer and saw something green. It was an alien! She was so surprised. It showed her that in a spaceship she didn't need a space suit while driving the spaceship. Then she went to a place that the alien did not like, it had a lot of bad aliens that stole a gem from the other aliens. So she decided to take it back on a mission. When she was on her first mission, she stole the gem. It triggered the alarm, and the aliens attacked Zara. Zara pressed a blinking button and it shot a wall of Legos. It was the coolest blaster ever. She went and completed other missions. She was the greatest space warrior ever.

MAGIC COOKIES

Mo is a person who really enjoyed cooking, mostly cookies. After baking them, she would pass them out to the neighbors. Everyone loved her cookies. One day everyone stayed home from work just waiting for her. Then they sadly left for work late because she didn't come. Mo was in her room watching a video that showed her how to make magic cookies. She made them and put them in the fridge for tomorrow morning. She didn't watch the very end that said "make sure to not ever put them in the fridge or else it will do the opposite thing. They were supposed to give you enough energy to last the whole day! The next morning Mo went around her neighborhood passing them out. When they ate them they could not move because they had no energy! The next day she baked the same type of cookies, but didn't refrigerate them. No one came to the door; she thought nobody liked the cookies. She went home and watched the video to the very end. She was so surprised she got the basket of cookies. Mo ran out the door and ran into everyone's house and fed them. They had enough energy to walk around and she was so happy.

SHORT TOWN

Hal is a man with a height of 6 feet 6 inches. He was tall and loved helping his family. One time he was going out to the cellar to get some oats. When he saw a lever, he opened it curiously. He saw a ladder, then he slipped off and fell into a ton of portals. When he stopped, he hit the ground. When he got up, he saw a ton of little men at about 4 feet 2 inches. Everything there was small. Hal asked a lot of the people there, but no one knew how to get back to earth. So he went to a huge hotel that was only 48 feet tall. Hal checked in and went to his room that was 5 feet tall. He hit his head on the ceiling. He didn't feel good, so he went to bed. He got up early the next morning and hit his head again. Hal was frustrated, so he went outside to stretch his neck. Then he realized he never asked the man at the front office. He ran back and hit his head again. Hal asked "Do you know how to get out of this place?" He hesitated then said "Yes, I do." Hal followed the midget; Hal saw the portal and jumped in. He was back in his world. Hal grabbed the oats and went back to the house. He was so happy to be back home!

THE POWER OF MUSIC

Brent is a man who really likes playing the bass guitar. He loved playing it so much he joined a band. He eventually opened his own guitar shop. There he would teach other people how to play the guitar. Brent taught so many people how to play and sold a lot of guitars. One time he went on a trip to Egypt to see some really cool pyramids! When he was walking through he saw a tiny engraving on a wall; it was some sort of song! He quickly wrote it down on some paper. When he got back, he grabbed a bass guitar and started playing the song. It was so soothing it could make him fly for a little bit. Brent then began saving people from falling off buildings. Brent was super proud of himself, but one day he realized he was the only one with that power. It made him feel bad, so he went outside and started a little fire and then burnt the paper. He was sad but happy. Then he went back to teaching. He knew he would never forget that song. His band also came to join him for dinner. He also had fun playing games with Timilie, the party mom.

BERNI'S DREAM

Remi is a baby who really wanted to walk. Every time something was near he used it to walk a little and exercise his legs. When he went to bed every night he dreamed of walking. One day when he woke up he decided he was going to walk. He got interrupted when he saw food; Remi loved food! He saw an apple and begged for it using actions, then he saw an egg. He was so hungry he started chewing on a cord. He was so mad he ruined a deck of cards. Remi was usually so happy but he really wanted food. Then he saw grapes. He was so hungry he grabbed his stuffed horse and tried to calm down. When it was breakfast time he was so happy. Remi loved his family so much. Then Remi remembered that he still had not learned how to walk. Then he got back to working on that. When the day was over he was so sad but the next day he crawled out of bed and out to the living room. Remi crawled over to a chair and started walking then fell and got up until he knew how to walk really well.

THE PARTY MOM

Timilie is a person who really likes to party. She went to parties all around the world. She partied in Hawaii, Egypt, and one of her favorite places to party was the United States of America. Timilie would party there for days and days. Sadly, the U.S. got tired of partying so they wouldn't let her come into the U.S.! She was so sad that she got rejected. Timilie wondered why they got tired of partying so she did some deep thinking about why they got tired of partying. She came to the conclusion that it just got old so she went to Egypt into a pyramid and went on a tour. In the pyramid, right next to a music engraving she found another engraving of things people really loved doing at parties. She went and got all these things and went to a random house. There she found a man burning a little fire. Timilie felt bad and threw a really big party. When the U.S. heard about this party they wanted to have more parties like Timilie's, and so she went home to the U.S.A. and had a ton of parties, especially with her family!

AGGRESSIVE ARIZONA

Shayla is a person who lived in the west. She loved it there. She rounded up cattle and branded them. She fed horses and rode them. Shayla was very active.

She had three dogs and a pet snake that she captured two months ago. Shayla loved Arizona and knew she would never leave. These are the three A's or AAA: Arizona, Aggressive, Active. Shayla made those up to go with the five C's; they are Cacti, Cattle, Copper, Citrus, and Cotton. She was very creative and smart. One day she was feeding the cows when her mom came out and told her that one of the horses escaped. Shayla went searching for a few hours. She couldn't find the horse until she saw something fast coming from the mountain, it was a bear! She still hadn't found the horse. Then she made a trail of hay leading to the pasture. Then she went to bed and the next morning the lost horse was in the pasture. Shayla was so happy she did her chores and went on a horse ride down at the bottom of Arizona.

SPACE ATTACK

Brenden is a person who really likes watching the stars. He was captured by aliens, but before we can tell you about that we have to tell you this. It started at school when Brenden got a letter with weird writing on it, but he threw it away not knowing what it was.

That night he went to go look at some stars when he saw a shooting star. The star hit Earth, and it was so cool he went to check it out. That's when he saw another shooting star that he went to look at. It turned out that the second one was a UFO. Brenden stood there watching it when something came out. He was a little scared when it came up to him. It was an alien; it was talking in a language not known on this earth. When Brenden replied, "I don't know what you're saying," the alien smacked him. Then he dragged him to the UFO and took off into space. Brenden stayed in space for two months. The alien wanted to take him to capture other humans, but he refused. The alien threw him in the UFO and flew to Earth. While they were headed towards Earth, Brenden got a space suit and a parachute and went straight into another planet! Right before he pressed the go button he jumped out and parachuted all the way to Earth.

ANIMAL HOUSE

Rafael is a man who loved animals. He owned almost every kind of animal. Rafael was not scared of any of them because he was able to communicate with them. He loved jelly fish but he also liked alligators. All his alligators were nice but one day he got a new alligator. This sounded like no big problem but it was, because this alligator was really bad. He would always tear up the furniture, eat all the food, and steal everything he could. Rafael tried to get the other alligators to help him be nice but it didn't work. He never got anything for Christmas except for coal, which he hated. One day he crossed the line when Rafael got home from work. That bad alligator had broken the door and the T.V. Rafael was so angry he sold the bad alligator and got a new one. After a while Rafael started to feel bad, so he planned what he was going to do. First he got online and looked at all the things he had ordered. He scrolled up and up until he found an alligator that looked like the mean one. Rafael bought it and when it got to his door he started to feel better and the alligator started to act nicer and they were all happy.

A GOOD DAY WITH NANA

Nana is a very nice lady. She loves cooking for others. She cooks stuff with Mo and her friends. Every Tuesday night she would go with her friends and play bingo or yahtzee. All of the other days she would spend with her family. One-day Nana woke up and made waffles which are super good, after that she made two new pillowcases for me. My nana is a great sewer, she sews the coolest things. After sewing a little she plays games with her family like Dutch Blitz and Egyption Rat Race. Those games are very fun, if you know how to play. Almost every day in the morning she will sit outside sometimes watching the world and sometimes she will read a book. After doing all these things she will take a nap. Then she will play more games like Trash and Qwixx. Then she will cook dinner which is always so good. Tonight we ate super nachos, everyone in our family loves super nachos. After we eat we play one more game called Wits and Wagers which is my favorite game. The last thing we do is get ready for bed and we go to sleep.

IMAGINATION

CPSIA information can be obtained
at www.ICGtesting.com
Printed in the USA
BVHW022349291121
622778BV00008B/711